Adrian Bowley, born on 30th January 1958 in Nottingham, is now a fully-fledged pensioner. He lives with his family in a small town between Derby and Nottingham, along with their adorable cocker spaniel, Peggy.

After 42 years of clerical work, Adrian suddenly had a lot more spare time on his hands. Luckily, they were first-time dog owners, which meant most of their leisure time was occupied with walking Peggy and keeping her out of mischief. This led to Adrian considering a journey into the world of short stories resulting in *'It's Raining Cats and Dogs'*.

Adrian Bowley

RAINING CATS AND DOGS

AUSTIN MACAULEY PUBLISHERS
LONDON * CAMBRIDGE * NEW YORK * SHARJAH

Copyright © Adrian Bowley 2025

The right of Adrian Bowley to be identified as author of this work has been asserted by the author in accordance with sections 77 and 78 of the Copyright, Designs and Patents Act 1988.

All rights reserved. No part of this publication may be reproduced, stored in a retrieval system, or transmitted in any form or by any means, electronic, mechanical, photocopying, recording, or otherwise, without the prior permission of the publishers.

Any person who commits any unauthorised act in relation to this publication may be liable to criminal prosecution and civil claims for damages.

This is a work of fiction. Names, characters, businesses, places, events, locales, and incidents are either the products of the author's imagination or used in a fictitious manner. Any resemblance to actual persons, living or dead, or actual events is purely coincidental.

A CIP catalogue record for this title is available from the British Library.

ISBN 9781035850280 (Paperback)
ISBN 9781035878321 (ePub e-book)

www.austinmacauley.com

First Published 2025
Austin Macauley Publishers Ltd®
1 Canada Square
Canary Wharf
London
E14 5AA

The inspiration for my manuscript was my family and our lovely cocker spaniel, "Peggy".

And friends for great ideas and support in so many ways.

tautology

badly →
expressed

Prologue

I think it's fair to say that I've never particularly been a "dog person".

In fact, one of the commonly used phrases now is whether you're a dog or a cat person.

Safe to say I don't think I dwell into either camp.

As a child, the only pets my brother and I had were hamsters.

One of these was called Chumpitaz, strangely named by my mother after "Hector Chumpitaz", a Peruvian footballer who represented his homeland in the World Cup.

Sadly, my mother has now passed away along with my father as well.

So other than feeding a couple of local "moggies" these were our only experiences with household pets.

What a transformation now as my brother and I have both become responsible dog owners.

In fact, my only real memories of dogs were when I was out on a training run for a half marathon or some other local athletic event. There were so many occasions when I was navigating a local field that a snappy little dog would chase after me and attach itself to my ankle.

It is also my recollection that the owner would cheerfully call out, "Don't worry. He's only playing."

Needless to say, my experiences of the canine breed weren't that positive.

So, with all this in mind, you may ask why would I eventually become an evolving dog owner, later in life.

Well…I have my family to thank for that.

So Why a Dog Now?

For so long, my wife and our kids, Ernest and Naomi, have been pestering me to get us all a dog, trying to convince me that what we needed to make the family complete was "a dog".

Bearing in mind my previous experiences with our canine friends, this still wasn't a proposal that filled me with as much joy as the rest of the household at No 8.

As far as I was still concerned, my main argument was, "Who would look after Fido when we were at work?" But this continued to fall on seemingly deaf ears. No matter what arguments you were presented with for this addition to our clan, I was always able to offer a counterargument in reply.

But as the years progressed, they gradually wore me down. As it transpired, I gradually reduced my working week, and with the kids showing real enthusiasm for future dog walks, how could I not begin to warm up to the idea?

If you also add in the availability of local doggy daycare establishments. How could I possibly put up any opposition? Doggy daycare was becoming a real growth industry and so I eventually agreed that it was time to choose a puppy.

She Chose Us

It may surprise you to hear that the closer the "puppy day" loomed, the more excited I became, it could be said that my levels of delirious excitement were very close to matching those of the rest of the family.

As we approached the farm, having done stringent homework on the establishment along with all the other requisite checks. It was fair to say that those same levels of excitement were now going stratospheric.

The young lady at the farm was extremely thorough in her description of all we needed to do, as well as going through any necessary paperwork. This was particularly important, especially for us as first-time dog owners. We were very grateful for her assistance.

So now all that remained was to be introduced to the cute cocker spaniel puppies and make our choice. Having said that, it soon became clear that it wasn't our choice to make.

Faced with this glorious collection of doe-eyed bundles of fur. One of them clearly stood out from the rest.

The one in question, we later learned was a girl, ventured out to see what all the commotion was about, and to give our son a lick on the face as he leaned over the enclosure.

From that special moment onwards, it became increasingly clear what a great decision we had made, notwithstanding the challenging moments that inevitably come with having a young exuberant puppy in the house. You certainly don't have to be too house proud, as a young dog tests your patience to the limit, with minor (or even major) damage to fixtures and fittings always a possibility.

We named her Peggy and so began the journey of us getting used to her, and Peggy getting used to us.

The early days of dog ownership became further complicated in 2018 when I suffered a serious knee injury after being knocked off my bike in a serious collision with a van on my way to work in July of that year.

Needless to say, I came off second-best in that one.

But the consequences of that were that extra dog walking duties had to be shared between the rest of the family, which they gladly took on with smiles on their faces.

Also, a big shout out to all dog walkers at local daycare centres.

As the years passed by with the awful pandemic, lockdowns and, for us personally, the tragic passing of Rebecca's mum and my parents in a short space of time, this obviously hit us all really hard.

Having said that, the one constant was the support of wonderful friends and other family members. Gradually, the daily routine of walking Peggy became ingrained in our lives, even in inclement conditions.

Although she was never quite so keen on the rain, she was a real beacon of light in what would otherwise have been dark, depressing times.

Gradually, strong bonds were formed between man and beast, as our four-legged friend soon became one of the family, providing so many memories to cherish.

But it was in the winter of 2023, that this perfect scenario was shattered by a dire set of events that threatened everything we held dear.

Alan

Well, the prelude to the dog walk through the housing estate and down the Twitchell (this may be called something different where you live) was the same as so many walks that preceded it.

What was different this morning was the glorious weather we had woken up to, a stark contrast to the turbulent conditions we previously had to endure. Perhaps today we could enjoy the four-mile hike along the lovely paths and nearby fields without interruption.

Of course, there was the normal palaver in trying to get Peggy's protective shoes on. We had been advised to get these by the vet as a way of preventing the lesions that occasionally formed on her front paws due to excess skin. These could also be made worse if she licked them continually. As a result, she sometimes had to wear protective socks if it became too much of a problem.

But what they didn't prepare us for was the excessive cost of said items only available on an exclusive website from a Parisian manufacturer.

How much? "Oh, for the love of dogs!"

Even so, Peggy had quickly become the "talk of the town" in her natty boots, which certainly added to her noble factor, attracting a horde of new admirers whenever we walked her down the town.

So, after the normal 13-minute battle to get her shoes on. We were finally ready having completed the statuary checklist.

Boots on	Check
Phone	Check
Inhaler	Check
Treats	Check
Poo Bags	Check

"Oh yes, and not forgetting the dog!"

So, as I said, we were finally setting course on the usual route.

For some reason, it was taking longer and more chicken treats to entice Peggy to get going. We still had to cross the railway bridge, and on to the sidings where the real walk would begin.

Peggy seemed more reluctant this morning. Occasionally planting her paws on the ground creating an immovable object.

Even so, inch by inch, step by step, and treat by treat, we were edging closer to the lush green vegetation where we could really get going.

The treats were disappearing at an alarming rate, and I was seriously beginning to doubt that I had stockpiled enough to reach our destination. Fortunately, once we had crossed the bridge, Peggy was off-lead. She did pick up the pace in search of the smell of rabbit. Only now did the seven km that she had done so many times become a genuine possibility.

Maybe next time I'll have to bring out half a pound of cheese as an extra inducement for her to get walking.

At that moment, I had a vivid memory of an incident that still makes me chuckle to this day. When still a puppy, Peggy had run through our open gate and escaped into the cul-de-sac. Much to the amusement of the neighbours, I started running around the street with what must have looked like a block of double Gloucester in an attempt to entice her back home. This has since gone down in Worrall Avenue folklore.

There was another possible explanation for Peggy's reluctance today. I'm sure she is not on her own in the animal kingdom for being able to pick up on changes in the atmosphere, and shifts in weather patterns.

Were her senses alert to such things this morning? Indeed, as I looked up it did appear that the previously blue sky was beginning to display signs of wispy clouds encroaching from the west.

Marlene

Well, is this what my life has come to?

The reality has finally hit me. My days will really end at this establishment, a nursing home only a couple of miles from where I spent 32 years with my husband, Frank. That lovely bungalow with such fantastic neighbours.

We'd spent so long making it our own, but how things can change just proves you should take nothing for granted in this world.

Terence, our son, thought it would be best for me to be looked after on a full-time basis. This was after the minor stroke I'd had a year ago. Although my speech was only slightly affected, it left me very frail. After a couple of falls I had suffered, possibly I was in the best place.

With due respect to our Terence, he was very busy; he had a high-powered job in the city. He'd never met anyone to settle down with, so it would appear that no grandchildren would be forthcoming. This continued to fill me with sadness, and I know the same could be said about Frank before he sadly passed.

Frank and I had a wonderful life before his Alzheimer's got a lot worse. At the time, he was on medication but it became clear it was too late as his condition had rapidly deteriorated to the point that even with full-time careers, his quality of life had become non-existent.

It had been at least four years since Frank had passed away and mentally, I was still on a downward spiral without my long-term friend and confidant.

I still talk to him in the morning in the quiet moments with an aching desire to have any sort of reply.

More and more, I was having forgetful moments. About things such as what I had for tea yesterday. But as is so often the case with this dreadful condition, my memories of the past were so lucid, enclosing me in a cosy ball of familiarity.

But as I stared wistfully from my favourite perch by the bay window, I began to give thanks for the few friends I had made in the home. One friend in particular was Joyce, who had been such a great source of comfort to me in the most difficult times.

Having said that, the home was a place where everyone supported each other in their own special way.

These and many other thoughts were going through my head as I reflected on the view before me. In a place like this, one certainly gets plenty of time to think.

Today, I was pondering about the gurgling of the water as it wound its way through the landscape. I remembered a programme about one of the world's rivers where the presenter followed it from its source high up in the overhanging mountains. It was very interesting.

From here, there were the distinct calls of ramblers and dog walkers mingling with the cheerful cries of youngsters on the nearby housing estate.

But amidst this idyllic scene, one other thing suddenly catches my gaze. Considering how bright and fresh the day had started, it did appear even through my slightly blurred vision that some of the encroaching clouds seemed to be increasing in size and number.

Although blue was still the sky's predominant colour. The clouds were a possible indication of the arrival of more changeable weather conditions.

Alan

From my point of view, I think it is really important to stress how sociable a pastime dog walking is.

As Peggy set off across the well-worn paths over Totton fields, I was beginning to wonder which of the other regulars Peggy and I would bump into. Although I have to admit that none of the humans' names are known to me. There are several doggy names I am familiar with. These include Vince the labradoodle, Derek the red setter, Maisel the Pomeranian, and a couple of cardigan corgis.

This is only the tip of the iceberg concerning dogs we have encountered on our travels. It always makes us chuckle when Peg engages one of her friends in a vigorous game of chase, or they both circle each other trying to sniff their respective posteriors. This doesn't take into account whether the other animal is agreeable or not.

The main point of this is that we are all part of an unofficial social club, ready to share news or any problems we have.

On this particular morning, the hitherto beautiful start to the day was slowly beginning to change.

Now, when it comes to dog walking, I am often accused by the rest of the family of being obsessed with the weather. I am always glued to whoever is delivering the forecast, be it national or local. I then delve into the deeper insights as displayed in the hourly breakdowns, and when exactly a splodge of blue is over the little town.

But of course, none of this is enough, as I also do regular checks on the weather app installed on my phone. Today, we have been promised scattered showers moving in from the west later according to my app, there was a 10% chance of a light shower at 11 am.

Hence, the odds should have been in my favour with a 10 am departure in near-perfect conditions.

This was further confirmed by the full sun with the gentle south-westerly breezes we were currently blessed with.

Well, on the face of it, this should have been a perfect walk so why was there a nagging doubt hedging into my subconscious?

So, rather than the route chosen for today, would a shorter visit to Squirrel Alley in the town park be a safer option? It offers greater opportunities to shelter against any unexpected precipitation.

This also gives Peggy a chance for an athletic workout, chasing her favourite quarry along the tree-lined areas where they are densely populated.

Still, it is what it is, as one major philosopher once said. Also, it seemed that this particular canine had overcome her reluctance to walk, judging by her enthusiastic ruffling through the undergrowth in search of prey.

In stark contrast to his dog's frenzied activity, blissfully ignorant of the change in weather, I was nowhere as near as confident of my surroundings.

As I glanced upwards, it seemed that the bright yellow orb in the sky was becoming ever hazier by the minute.

Marlene

Uncomfortable thoughts were going through my mind as my attention was once again focused on the grounds of the home and fields just beyond. What else was there to do in this place on a Tuesday morning? One day of the week when no social events were planned on the calendar.

The morning had dawned with such a refreshing change to the turbulent weather that had hit the east midlands. They had labelled it a mild winter, and if by that you mean, wet, windy, dank, and miserable with constant flooding, then indeed mild did cover it.

But today, there had even been a slight frost at dawn, and we had seen very few of those this winter.

Suddenly, I was aware of an eerie silence as there was a shift in the atmosphere. Was this a precursor to more disturbing conditions? The number of clouds was certainly increasing.

Oh no! Could rain be on the way? Yet Again?

At first, clouds in the sky were beginning to outnumber the blue as greys and purples were increasing, threatening to completely cover the blanket of blue, which was predominant about half an hour ago.

With all this in mind, I wasn't completely surprised to hear a faint, almost indistinct rumble of the thunder in the distance. As yet, it was but a gentle drumbeat in the heavens, almost as if the orchestra was just warming up, unbeknownst to everyone. I was also pondering the words of the weather forecast.

The latest display now showed the possibility of scattered thunderstorms but as they always say in a chirpy, singing voice, *"These will be hit and miss."*

I then began to think of meteorological jargon.

Most people would be lucky and miss them altogether but if you get caught in one, you'll certainly know about it.

Well, at least I'm indoors.

Alan

By the look of the sky in this neck of the woods, it looked as if Peggy and I were going to be among those unfortunate souls who would be caught up in a "hit and miss" thunderstorm.

I then made the executive decision that the best option would be to turn around and get back home as soon as possible. Thinking of home, I wondered if Rebecca was watching one of her old favourites, *'Place in the Sun'* a reality TV show. It was a programme where the experts helped people buy a home in a warm, sunny location turning a dream into a reality!

Just as I was pondering something like that for Rebecca and I, the first drops of rain began to fall.

My original decision was now endorsed further as our trusty spaniel began to cast anxious-looking glances in my direction. Assuming that an animal's state of mind can be judged from their expression. Dogs normally trust our instincts completely so it appeared we were unanimous.

"Home it is," I turned to her and said. "Okay, Peggy, let's get home before it gets too bad."

Even though she responded immediately, neither of us could have been prepared for the speed of the incoming storm.

I was really surprised at how fast Peggy picked up the pace. Also, there was no need to guide her where to go as her in-built Sat-Nav was set for NG10 INR, our compact but bijou semi-detached on the outskirts of town.

I was struggling to keep up with her, and with only two kilometres to cover, we should reach the safe haven of home very soon and also make sure the rest of the family was alright.

Unfortunately, the incoming weather event had other ideas, as the accompanying wind had changed from a gentle to a moderate breeze and the previously light rain was now becoming a steadier and heavier drizzle.

As if that wasn't enough, I could now hear loud thunderclaps, which seemed to be coming from all directions.

Peggy's reaction to thunder was consistent as she began to bark incessantly at the noises from above.

Just then, we were stopped in our tracks as the nearby park was fully illuminated by an amazing bolt of forked lightning, which seemed to hit the earth far too close for comfort. Then it was as if a light switch had turned down and they were once again plunged into near darkness. This was a surreal moment for 11 am.

Peggy and I were stopped in our tracks, not knowing where to turn or what to do.

I could not believe how quickly this tempest (for there was no other word for it) had approached and now engulfed us. "Peg, we need to shelter, fast!" I cried as my fear level was going off the scale. I was absolutely drenched in a short space of time, and Peggy was just a ball of dripping wet fur. Indeed, my concern was reserved for the innocent and vulnerable pooch entrusted to my care.

But where to take shelter? The scientific advice is to never take refuge under a tree in conditions such as these, but we needed to find somewhere as the thunder and lightning fizzed and cracked all around us. Not to mention the increasing volume of the wind and the relentless rain.

Peggy and I had been in some tight spots before but we had never been faced with conditions as horrific as these.

Marlene

By now, I was being treated to a pyrotechnic display. The like of which I had never seen in all my 84 years.

It was frightening, and yet spellbinding and exciting at the same time. I was glued to the bay window as the forces of nature were being played out before me.

The thunderclaps were increasing in volume even more. Seemingly to fever pitch. The storm now seemed to be directly overhead. The space in time between the thunder and lightning was getting shorter and shorter.

I did recollect my parents or an elderly friend once giving me some advice on this subject. I was told to count between the crash of thunder and the ensuing lightning. As far as my memory serves me, five seconds equated to the storm being one mile away. This was extremely close as I didn't even manage to count to four.

But all this activity was merely the prelude to a monsoon-like downpour causing water to stream down the window like a torrent.

But strange as it sounds, the wind seemed to have lost a little of its ferocity. Was I mistaken or were the window panes not rattling as they were a few minutes ago?

Another indication of how strong the wind was came from the fact that the double glazing had only been installed two years ago. But even as the wind was decreasing ever so slightly, other sounds were now fighting for her attention.

Unless my ears were playing tricks on me...

Was that a faint human cry and? No, it can't be... no... the muted bark of a dog? Surely, that's not possible. It is very faint but who would have ventured out on a day like this?

"Who knows, what danger they could be in?"

I was musing on all this as I strained my hearing to make sure I was hearing what I thought I was hearing.

Alan

If Marlene was getting a ringside seat, undercover, the best seat in the house to witness the spectacle of the last storm to hit the UK this winter, then Alan and Peggy were directly in the firing line of what was later described by the experts as a "Once in a lifetime storm".

The fact that we were now on the letter "G" in the alphabet of named storms was a perfect illustration, if any was still needed, of how turbulent this winter had been.

Unfortunately, this particular low pressure that had been predicted to remain to the west of the UK, had decided to take a little detour towards us where its presence was certainly being felt by anyone on its path.

The storm certainly brought to mind another incident when our Ernest, normally a heavy sleeper, had been awakened by thunder that he could only describe as the sound of 100 wheelie bins being dropped on the roof from a great height.

By now, I should have realised that the tree we were sheltering under was offering no protection whatsoever from the current downpours of biblical portions. It certainly felt as if the well-publicised effects of climate change were being displayed here in this small British town.

I have heard it said that even when faced with extreme danger, the individual is still able to focus on past events, especially those that evoke similar emotions.

But the moments that came to me at this time were the numerous times that Peggy had disappeared into the woods in pursuit of her arch-enemy.

"Eastern grey squirrel" also known as "sciurus carolinensis". On each occasion, she was completely oblivious to the worry and anxiety of whoever was walking her at the time. But each time youthful exuberance got the better of our cocker spaniel as once again she would be oblivious to our frustration, pleased for her to come back.

I do recall one never-to-be-forgotten episode when my exasperation reached such a level that I completely lost it and launched the extendable lead with such a force that it skidded along the greasy surface and promptly landed in the local brook.

To this day, I have no idea of how I got the "pesky pooch" home.

Although, these were amusing anecdotes to share with family and friends. I do recall one particularly scary episode that was fraught with danger.

Although not weather-related, this was an incident that caused my fear level to be almost comparable to the current situation.

The occasion I am thinking of was when Peggy suddenly took it upon herself to go flying up a steep slope, leaving me with no choice but to go chasing at her.

As I pursued her, I lost my footing and would have plunged into the abyss (well at least 40 feet in this instance) had I not managed to grab hold of a prickly gorse bush. Which luckily broke my fall.

So there I was, a 60-year-old man, with absolutely no hiking experience and none of this requisite safety equipment, suddenly facing what appeared to be a real life and death situation. On top of that, I still had to locate a floppy-eared dog.

After what was a tortuous and extremely painful uphill scramble. I finally stood a gasping, wheezing wreck at the summit, covered in cuts and bruises from the ordeal.

Then commenced some maniacal blundering in the bushes as I vainly began the search for the priceless family pet. There was simply no way I could return home and how would I explain that "Sorry, I've lost the dog"?

Imagine my relief when just as my cries were getting ever more frantic, I caught sight of a panting bundle of fur under a large bush.

Bet you won't run off like that again, Pegs!

Come to think of it, I think she did run off again a week later.

It was at this point that my attention was jerked back to the present. In abject horror, I found myself staring at my empty hand. The lead was not there along with our Peggy.

I began to shout, "Peg, Peg, get here now. Where are you, Peggy?"

Embarrassingly, I was too afraid to let go of the tree I was still clinging to for dear life.

The fear that we had seen the last of her, really did surface this time.

Then, just as I was more panic-stricken, I sensed, rather than heard a slight whimpering, but from where I couldn't fathom.

Once again I shrieked out, "Stay there, Peg. I'll come and get you as soon as I can."

Unfortunately, Peggy was too afraid to venture from her safe space and I remained helpless and literally rooted to the spot.

I was getting more and more distraught about what I would tell the wife and kids if I came back without our friend. I always assumed, of course, that I could get out of this mess myself.

I was still clinging onto the tree for dear life when I suddenly heard a low creak accompanied by a terrible wrenching noise.

It was at that point that the earth began to move beneath my feet.

Marlene

Even above the cacophony of the storm that was raging, I could still occasionally hear the cries of desperation but they did seem to be getting more discernible and louder. They appeared to be carrying towards me on the moderate breeze, still evident from the swaying in the nearby trees.

But the barks I could hear previously had now completely disappeared, even during the lulls that were starting to appear between the many violent outbursts of the storm. There was now the odd glimmer of hope as there were signs of the worst of it blowing over. But no doubt, it could still have a sting in its tail.

All of this brought a particular memory back to me as the rain began to pour from the gutters.

I was transported back to a wonderful holiday I had with Frank to celebrate our 30th wedding anniversary.

We spent a wonderful few days in a lovely hotel, just a stone's throw away from Niagara Falls.

The highlight of the stay was the chance to experience, at first hand, the cascading waters of the falls from our vantage point on the "Maid of the Mist".

Frank and I have been so blessed to go on some of the holidays, we really have seen some amazing sights in this world of ours. I still long for those days.

But as for this storm, it did seem that as quickly as it had arrived. The rain did seem to be slowing to a heavy drizzle, and there was a significant reduction in the volume of the thunderclaps. Based on my previous hypotheses of the thunder and lightning. Dare we even hope that the storm was moving away?

But as things quietened down on the storm front. This allowed the desperate ones, whoever was in the nearby field, to become even more audible.

Suddenly, the realisation hit me that I needed to do something rather than just remain a helpless bystander. *But what?* I asked myself. First of all, I need to remain calm and oh yes! There's an emergency number on my mobile.

Luckily, our Terence had given me a short tutorial on how it worked and what it could do. So, I was ready for action.

I duly pressed the right button and was routed through to an "emergency services operative".

Alan

Meanwhile, things were about to get a lot worse for our hapless dog walker. The preceding monsoon, which was still falling intermittently had swollen this particular tributary of the Erewash, by now it was straining at its leash to burst its banks.

In a very weird moment I turned to poetic verse , reliving the day so far up to the predicament I now found myself in. Under such pressure, surprisingly the words soon flowed,

Man and Dog set off in the morning Sun,
To a day full of promise, and who knows what fun.
All preparations made and a cheery Goodbye,
Clouds having parted to reveal a welcome blue sky.
After a stubborn, sluggish start Peggy soon picks up the trail,
How on earth could we possibly fail.
Why did moments of doubt suddenly appear in his head,
Knowing what could happen would have filled him with dread.
The sway of the trees seemed stronger than ever,
We need to stay close,
We need to stay together.
Dark clouds soon appear from the West,

Perhaps turning back would surely be best.
But convincing this Dog would be a completely different matter,
As large drops of rain began to pitter and patter.
But the crash up above caused this canine head to raise,
How on earth could this be happening, on today of all days.
Thunder soon began to rumble emitting a frightening sound,
As lightning lit up the fields from the air to the ground.
How quickly lashed the rain through our refuge in the tree,
Faced with such an onslaught, our canine chose to flee.
As I cried into the Tempest, all hope it seemed was lost,
Save us from this horror as our lives it will surely cost.

Peggy, Peg, Where are You?

It can't end like this,

Peggyyyyyyyyyyyyyyÿyyyy!!!!!!!!!!!!!!

Hello, Caller, Which Service Do You Require?

Marlene:

"I'm not sure. I've never done this sort of thing before. My Terence would know what to say, he's great at this sort of thing."

Operator:

"Don't worry, caller. Just take it slowly. I'm here to help you. All we need is a few details so we can get the help to where it is needed.

"Can we start with your name, please? And also, where you're calling from, if that's okay."

Marlene:

"Sorry, I'm all flustered. I think I've heard cries for help from the back of the home. You probably think I'm barking mad.

"Anyway, sorry, my name is Marlene. As far as I know, I was named after…Marlene Dietrich, but you probably don't need to know that. Oh! I think I heard a dog as well."

Operator:

"That's better, Marlene. I can call you Marlene, can't I?"

Marlene:

"That's absolutely fine. By the way, what's your name, my dear? You sound very friendly."

Operator:

"Thank you, Marlene, we do try and by the way my name is Sylvia. Can I start by saying you've done exactly the right thing by calling us today?

"Now, I just need to ask you a few more questions."

Marlene:

"Fire away, Sylvia, I think I'm getting the hang of this now. As I probably said, I'm pretty sure I've heard someone who needs help and sounds in a lot of distress."

Sylvia:

"I totally get that, Marlene, but we just need to know where to send some help to."

Marlene:

"BUT THEY NEED HELP NOW!"

Sylvia:

"Please, calm down, Marlene. We can't send help if we don't know where to send someone.

"So please, could you give me your address?"

Marlene:

"Sorry for shouting. I'm calling from Parkside Flats, Riverside Way, Totton.

"The shouts were coming from the fields at the back. Presumably, you'll have my mobile number from this call. I remember that people can do that."

Sylvia:

"We do indeed have your number, Marlene.

"Are you still there, caller? Stay on the line, please. Oh no! I think I've lost her."

Marlene:

"Oh no! I think I've pressed something. Sylvia, Sylvia, can you still hear me?"

Sylvia:

"Phew! I've got her back now take this slowly, Marlene. Did you say Totton with two Ts?"

Marlene:

"Yes! Yes! I did!"

(This time shrieking hysterically)

"But you're breaking up. This looked so much easier. On ambulance."

Sylvia:

"Geoff, sounds like someone needs the local rescue team but she keeps cutting out. She was back now we have all that.

"Marlene, now I have really lost her."

Alan

Strange what thoughts come into your head when you are clinging on to a tree for dear life, whilst being assailed in all directions by gusty winds and driving rain. Obviously, such thoughts are driven by panic and stress from the perilous position one finds oneself in.

Luckily, what had felt like a shift in the ground had now stabilised for a while but I was still hoping and praying that the roots of the tree, which now that I studied more closely, was nothing more than a medium-sized sapling, would hold firm until the rain abated. *Were these to be my last thoughts on this earth and was I now close to delivering my own personal eulogy?*

I began to ponder the wonderful marriage Rebecca and I had enjoyed up to his point. There was the joy of the kids and what they had grown up to be living in the same house for 37 years. When I say grown up. Ernest could still be a bit silly at times. But we love them both warts and all.

When it came to work and helping to provide for my family, I had spent 28 enjoyable years working for a major pharmaceutical company before taking a very acceptable voluntary redundancy package 18 years ago.

I do recall that the next redundancy situation at the optical retailer I worked for, was a completely different "kettle of fish".

The place itself never reached the dizzying heights of my previous employer but it did bring home the bacon for nearly 13 years.

The redundancy in questions happened in 2019, when I and another lady, slightly older than me were called into individual meetings with an HR person, which was never a good sign.

Anyway, to cut a long story short, we were basically told to pack our bags and get out of town.

Along with so many other families, the next three years were extremely difficult. Coupled with my own fruitless search for work, the global pandemic, and lockdowns, I suddenly realised what was staring me in the face.

I think I've retired.

Sadly, in the course of those three years, we lost Rebecca's mum and both of my parents after numerous hospital and care home visits.

This was a testing time for both of us, leaving very little time to think about work.

"Hold on, probably we're both retired."

Based on ensuing inheritances and our frugal lifestyle, in the words of Gloria Gaynor, *'We will survive'*.

But still, the loss of three loved ones in a short space of time hit our and Ruth's sisters' family really hard.

Still, as pensioners, we would have a lot more time for dog walking.

Talking of dogs, *Where's our Peggy and where's my phone?* How can I let the family know what is happening?

It was at that point I became aware of the rapidly rising water.

Perhaps it is time for a rendition of *'We All Live In a Yellow Submarine'*.

Marlene

I had been very nervous when making that call to emergency services. I was really hoping and praying that they had the right information, and that a team of rescuers were on the way to help that poor man and his dog. They did say they had a dedicated team for this sort of work. I was not going to leave this spot until I saw some sort of action out there.

The conversation had passed in a blur and the pleas for help were getting more and more desperate.

But thankfully, the rain had now slowed to a mere drizzle and the previously high decibel count of the thunderclaps was now almost non-existent. But where could all that rain go? Especially as the warning was for more localised flooding, the rain falling on already saturated surfaces. This was an accumulation of previous deluges but fortunately this one was more short lived.

Hold on! What's that noise I can hear? It is like a whooshing sound from the brook just over there. I had never heard that before. Normally, all you could hear was a calm freckle if the winds were in the right direction. Now it sounds anything but calm, my ears were indeed not deceiving me. The shallow tributary had suddenly become a stream and now a full-flowing river owing to the amount of water that had been poured into it.

I then realised that the eerie sound of gushing water did not augur well for anyone unfortunate enough to be in the vicinity.

I then had a terrible feeling about the proximity of those cries for help in relation to the angry-sounding water. This did make me even more concerned for their safety. *Come on, Marlene, it may be time to don that sou'wester and your Wellingtons and to go investigate.*

Alan

So, this normally benevolent stream, perhaps not even a stream but just a brook in its normal state, was now almost full to bursting. Venting its fury on everything in its wake, and in this case, poor Alan was also a victim caught up in the flow.

The shift that I had previously detected beneath my feet was now no longer holding firm as it suddenly turned into a mini landslide, and the main trunk of the tree suddenly detached itself from where it previously stood for many years.

For a moment, it seemed inevitable that I would dislodge completely from my place of refuge but in absolute desperation, there was one large overhanging branch I managed to cling onto. Currently, this was all that was preventing me from plunging into the swirling waters.

This set my pulse racing as I thought about how the level of water could rise so quickly in this particular stretch.

I remembered that, until recently, this area was home to the annual duck race, usually held on New Year's Day. A strange event where up to 300 ducks—not real, plastic ones, of course—were released from a bridge further upstream.

The said ducks were all numbered, allowing the spectators to buy a duck with all proceeds going to charity. There was a prize for the person who bought the first duck to cross the line.

Even in the predicament, I found myself thinking about it and couldn't help but chuckle at the thought of how quickly the ducks would have sped to the finishing line today.

In the meantime, flood water was still continuing to rise. Suddenly, I had a vision of being stuck in an oversized bathtub clinging onto a large tap that was pouring water in, at a quite prodigious rate. Of course, there was no escape and the contents of the tub were threatening to engulf me completely.

Was I going delusional? Was I losing my sanity? Well, what I did know was that I didn't think I could hang on for much longer.

I even had a forlorn hope that Peggy had run for help and that my rescuers would appear over the horizon.

This would be reminiscent of the dog Lassie in the old black-and-white movies. That's a blast from the past.

All of this was, of course, in vain as my trusted canine companion was still nowhere to be seen. Poor thing must have been really spooked to have disappeared like this.

I began to shout to the heavens, which was still very threatening but whose purple hues were at least showing signs of becoming a little fainter.

But this was my only crumb of comfort as the turbulent waters still frothed around me, now seemingly intent on dragging me under. Occasionally, my head disappeared only to reappear a few seconds later, causing me to gurgle, splutter, and spit out a mouth full of brown sludgy liquid.

Now I have heard it said that in certain desperate situations when a person's back is really up against the wall, they may turn to God for Divine intervention.

This may be family life and death situations or if they are facing severe problems from which they can see no possible solution. Such prayers are uttered whether or not people believe in God and whoever was addressed or not.

But I was a Christian with a strong faith, and I now turned to the God that I truly believed in. Inspired by the way that Jesus calmed the storm, I began to pray earnestly for man and beast. It was easily the most incoherent prayer I had ever uttered but I truly believed that my petitions would be answered.

I continued to babble away, especially for the safe delivery of my beloved Peggy.

Probably worth other shouts as well.

"Peggy, Peggy, I'm here, girl. We will be okay!"

Marlene

Meanwhile, back at the complex, I was still hearing the ongoing cries of distress coming from the fields occasionally.

I had tried to venture outside in my all-weather gear but I was told to turn back by the on-duty carer, who advised me to leave it to the professionals.

But where were the professionals?

It had been 40 minutes since my call and still, nothing seemed to be happening.

Then, out of the blue, I thought I could hear the piercing, shrill sound of a distant whistle, struggling to make itself heard over the still-high volume of the ebbing storm.

Dare I hope that my call had reached receptive ears and help really was on its way?

Alan

Even though the storm now seemed well past its height of intensity, it was clear from the huge pools of water on the field that the river would take a few days to shrink back to anything like its previous levels. Presumably, there would be a flood alert or even warning for this and other tributaries nearby.

I was still clinging on to the overhanging branch, my head still bobbing up and down, causing me to think the next breath I took could be my last.

Is this really how my life is going to end, on a perfectly straightforward dog walk, separated from his faithful friend of 5 years?

Had I also seen the last of my family? My wife Rebecca, Ernest and Naomi.

I hadn't had the chance to properly tell them how much I loved them, just a cheerio, see you later as I walked out this morning.

Even though Ernest and Naomi were 30 and 34 respectively, the housing market was still an elusive target for them both, especially in such difficult financial circumstances.

Although at least we did have perfect live-in dog sitters. Whenever Rebecca and I fancied a jaunt abroad or a long theatre weekend in the city.

Such were the perks of being carefree pensioners with more than adequate rainy day funds set aside, albeit one accumulated through inheritances—a sad consequence of my mum, dad, and Ruth's mum dying in a cruelly short space of time.

But then, just as my situation seemed to be drawing to its inevitable conclusion, another sound reached my ears just as I was about to have another chat with the man upstairs.

The sound in question was the piercing sound of a whistle, and not too far away by the sounds of it.

But if my ears were deceiving me, surely my eyes couldn't be blurred as they were from losing my varifocals when I slipped into the water.

I was sure that I could vaguely see the bobbing of lights from the next field along with indistinct shapes of what I really hoped were high-vis jackets.

"Over here! I'm over here! Help!"

He Is Over Here

"Help! Help!" I shouted. "I need help! Please."

Although my vision was impaired by the loss of my glasses, my hearing seemed to be compensating for that as I once again heard a muffled woof and a desperate whimpering. Where it was coming from I couldn't tell, but it didn't sound too far away.

"Keep calm, girl! Keep calm! We would be home for lunch soon."

It was not long before there was a sound of boots heading my way. I have never been so relieved in all my life.

"Phil, Mick, I've found him. He's over here. Bring the rope."

Then the most wonderful vision I had ever seen was suddenly before me.

Torch light was shone into my eyes and several people in high-vis jackets were imploring me to calm down.

"Stay still, mate, we've got this. We're here to help."

"What's your name, mate?"

"Alan," I replied. "But my dog, Peggy, is still missing."

"Don't worry, Alan, we'll find her as well. But we need to get you out first."

As luck would have it, the sky was gradually getting a little brighter and surely this lifting of the weather could only help in the rescue process.

"Now then, Alan, we need you to stay calm while we get ready to pull you out."

"Keep calm! Keep calm! I said…I'd like to see you keep calm when your neck is in flood water."

Although it was at that moment, when in trying to put my legs down, that I suddenly realised I could just about put my feet on the bottom, it looked like I might get out of this alive.

Even so, the flood water was still pummelling my body, leaving me with an intense desire for my feet to be on dryland. I had seriously had enough of this water by now. On the positive side, the rain had relented quite a bit… and the branch I was clinging to was, for the time being, keeping me afloat.

I have heard it said that it is possible to drown even in shallow water. So although help was at hand. I was not out of the woods yet.

Thankfully in no time, at all my rescuers were kitted up and ready for action. They reassured me that in their line of work. This would be a pretty run-of-the-mill scenario.

Pete, the leader, threw me a rope. Telling me to grab hold.

After what felt like the umpteenth time. I finally managed to summon the confidence to swap my branch for the new lifeline now being offered.

"Farewell, old branch, I'm outta here."

Pete and three other members of the team began to pull manfully on the other end of the rope. I felt the river gradually slip away behind me.

Even with my impaired vision, I could see the grass on the fields getting closer. The next thing I knew, I was spluttering in relief as several pairs of hands reached out and pulled me the last few meters to safety.

Waves of exhaustion engulfed me. Threatening to overcome me completely as I tried to stand upright. Indeed, I would have slipped back again if not for those same pairs of hands grabbing me again, pulling me back onto Terra firma. Blimey, was my ordeal finally over? I tried to squint my eyes to take in the scene before me.

"Step away from the edge, mate."

Someone said, and I duly obliged the order to sit awhile and compose myself.

I moved away and crouched down in a state of shock and what was later confirmed as mild hysteria. When my thoughts finally became a bit more lucid, they eventually turned to a certain orange roan cocker spaniel and where Peggy was.

I suddenly shouted, "She's about so high four legs big, floppy ears with orange blotches on a white background. Someone must have seen her."

"Settle down, lad," another member of the team said. "She can't have gone far, she'll have just taken cover and scared out of her wits, we'll find her."

Pete suddenly chimed in, "Remember that labrador we rescued last week on the other side of town? It was stuck, too afraid to move until we coaxed it out with a bit of chicken, speaking of which, anybody got any chicken on them or even a bit of cheese."

Then, as if on cue, the most wonderful sound could be heard. Whether or not it was the words Peggy had heard or not, who knows, but there was a sudden incessant barking that reverberated joyfully around the fields.

I immediately gave thanks as I recognised the bark straightaway and at the same time, the sun peeked its way through the clouds, revealing a huge patch of blue sky that was amazing to behold.

Having said that, for me, it was still a little fuzzy around the edges.

Marlene

As the horrendous storm seemed to have finally passed over, I once again was considering going outside to see what was happening on the fields.

I had heard a bit of a commotion outside and judging from the faces of her inmates, it rather looked as if I had been elected as the representative to go outside and see what all the noise was about. That is if I was allowed to venture from home this time.

The other residents were more than happy to remain indoors knowing that their friend would give them a full report on her return.

Doreen, the complex manager, wasn't too happy about me going out, but as the countryside was now bathed in sunshine, she relented.

Although Doreen did warn me to be extremely careful as it could still be a bit treacherous. Underfoot. She was still afraid of what would meet her as once again she prepared herself.

Hopefully, not too much damage would have been vented on the normally serene surroundings.

The complex manager fully understood that Marlene wanted to know about the repercussions of her phone call.

Luckily, I'd still got that all-weather gear although, by the looks of it, I may not need it now. What I will need are my all-terrain boots, which take me back to the long walks that Frank and I enjoyed in the high peak.

There was one amazing walking holiday that we undertook in the Austrian Tyrol, the views that we had witnessed will remain with me until my dying day.

I approached the group of men in high-vis jackets with a little trepidation, completely unaware of how I was allowed to progress any further.

I introduced myself to the person who seemed to be in charge, he told me his name and the names of a few of his team. They also told me the name of the man they had rescued. Apparently, his name was Alan but he was still suffering from shock especially as his dog still hadn't been located.

I told them it was me who had made the call and it made me chuckle when Francesca, one of the two female members of the crew, told me I could well be in line for a "Pride of Britain Award".

I decided to leave them to it and started to head back to await further developments.

"What a lovely lady," Pete said. "And at least we have her number to tell her when Alan's dog is found."

Just as I turned around, I noticed a man huddled down with a space blanket around him, I took this to be Alan.

One of those gathered told him that it was me who made the call that had probably saved his life.

He gave me an enormous hug, and couldn't stop telling me how thankful he was and that he wouldn't be here talking to me if it hadn't been for my 999 call.

Just at that moment, we were disturbed by a real commotion from a patch of nearby foliage.

At the sight before us, we both gasped inwardly and him even without his glasses.

Alan knew what he was witnessing, I think my smile was almost as broad as Alan's and what one must rate as one of the happiest moments in my life.

Alan

All of sudden there was a parting of the bushes about a hundred yards away from where I had been pulled from the water.

Then, quite miraculously, one of the rescuers emerged with something white and orange in his hands.

"Look at what I've found in the undergrowth," said Mohammed as he was clearly struggling to hold a squirming wriggling 18 kg of cocker spaniel.

(According to the vets she still had a kilogram to lose, the family would probably have to cut down on her cheese allowance).

Even though the poor thing was be draggled and windswept, her normally grumpy face was immediately transformed into a broad, beaming smile when she caught sight of her owner. She bounded over to me and delivered a big smacker of a kiss. She also let Marlene give her lots of fuss as well. This was one overjoyed cocker spaniel.

Marlene then felt that it was the right time to leave Peggy and I to enjoy their emotional reconciliation.

My world was transformed from one of stress and anxiety to one of joy and ecstasy at being reunited with my fluffy-eared buddy. I gave thanks that my prayers had been answered.

The effect it had on everyone present was unbelievable and there wasn't a dry eye in the house as grown men and women were reduced to blubbering wrecks. They later described the emotion of the event as something they had never witnessed before.

Not long after this, blue flashing lights appeared in the nearby cul-de-sac that had seen so much drama in the preceding hour. After some standard checks, I was cleared for transfer to the local AeE, after insisting very strongly that Peggy will be allowed to travel with me.

Jan, one of the paramedics was not sure of the protocol but after a chat with her shift buddy, Peggy was allowed to jump on board.

Once we were on our way to the local hospital, my details were taken, especially those of my nearest and dearest so that they could be informed where to meet us shortly. I was further reassured by the fact that an in-house vet would also be on hand to give Peggy the once-over as well.

Arrival at AeE was such a relief that Peggy had to be physically prised away from my side. Only then could we be examined and the quicker that happened the quicker we could get back to no 8.

Not long after we got to the hospital, Rebecca, Ernest, and Naomi burst into our cubicle. There followed endless hugs and a certain canine got the most fussing one of his breeds had ever received.

"We have been calling you and calling you," they all said, obviously unaware that I was in no position to return their calls.

Peggy was quite happy to roll onto her back for some customary belly rubs and a new packet of her favourite salmon sticks was opened to mark the occasion.

She then entertained us all by running around the ward with a pair of medical overshoes in her mouth. This probably breached so many hospital regulations, but the staff were laughing far too much, to be fair, it was providing entertainment for the other patients as well.

It was only a couple of hours after we'd arrived, that we were given the green light to say goodbye and return home. By then, we had both showered and made ourselves a lot more presentable to the wider world. Especially in a fresh change of clothes that Rebecca had bought in. It was also good to be able to see things a lot more clearly thanks to my spare pair of glasses, once again kindly supplied by my lovely wife.

I felt a lot fresher but by no means back to 100%. On the other hand, Peggy was not quite so happy at having to take a bath. We all thought she looked clean and beautiful, but the problem was she was still a little damp.

Then much to the horror of all the doctors and nurses on the ward. The little rascal went bonkers trying to rub herself dry on the sheets of the nearby bed, luckily unoccupied at the time, once again we were in hysterics until Peggy slumped on the floor. Fixing us with a look of utmost disgust. I think they'll be glad to see the back of us.

But we couldn't leave without thanking everyone for what they had done, including two of the brilliant rescue team members who had stayed behind to make sure we were alright. They accepted our grateful thanks on behalf of all the lads and lasses who had saved us from a terrible fate.

I was still feeling a bit out of sorts and slightly traumatised from the ordeal. I was offered and gratefully accepted some counselling sessions to treat the PTSD which would inevitably result from my ordeal. Luckily, dogs appear fully equipped to bounce back from such experiences.

But in the short term, I know what's good for shock, a little nip of my favourite malt, whisky. With that in mind, I poured myself a generous measure, plonked myself in my favourite armchair and began to relive the dog walk that almost ended in tragic circumstances.

Actually, one more glass wouldn't harm, would it?

I asked Rebecca to take the bottle away as it was beginning to slide down a little too easily.

Thanks

When the dust was finally beginning to settle. I was reminded of the phone call that had saved Peggy and I from serious injury or even loss of life. I realised I had to do one more thing before we all settled down for our evening meal. Luckily, Marlene and I had swapped details before I got in the ambulance. Now then, where did I put her mobile number?

The restaurant would have to be dog-friendly.

Marlene was absolutely overjoyed and couldn't wait to invite Joyce, or possibly Doug and Elsie as well.

Her infectious laughter set off, although I did say there may not be room at the restaurant for the whole nursing home.

"Sorry, Alan," she said. "I got a bit carried away there."

"Bye, Marlene," I replied. "I'll let you know all the arrangements tomorrow."

Marlene could not wait to dig into her glad rags for such an occasion, something she very rarely got to do.

She couldn't wait to tell Terrance and have a quiet word with Frank later on.

Marlene

Meanwhile, back at home, I was sitting in my favourite chair with a cup of strong tea with two sugars and a plate of garibaldi biscuits.

What a day this has been, I thought, as I ran over all the events that have happened since I got up this morning, munching on a delicious bacon butty with brown sauce.

It gave me a warm inner glow, thinking of the phone call that had led to the rescue of that lovely chap and his faithful dog, I was so pleased to hear from the hospital how relieved the family were when they saw each other again.

But anyway, back to more important matters,

I now had a lovely meal to look forward to with my lifelong friend Joyce and the Bonley family.

I was quite certain that through what happened today, I had made some friends for life and, as they say on reality TV, *'It's been a journey'.*

Hopefully, it is just the beginning of a journey of friendship with this lovely group of people.

Talking of family, Frank told me he was really proud of what I had done today, and before I forget, I must ring Terence and fill him in on the details.

Now then, on to important matters as I scanned my wardrobe.

Will it be the peach trouser suit, or the long.?

Floaty purple number.

Decisions, decisions.

I think I'll have to sleep on it.

Meanwhile, at No 8

There was one particular cocker spaniel that was ready for a long overdue Scooby snack, a slap-up dinner, or both even judging by her longing looks at the drawer that contained her dried food. We should better feed her quick.

In fact, her imploring face was clearly expressing the words.

"Feed me! Feed me now!"

Even though she'd had more treats than normal from the nurses at the hospital, who had clearly taken her to their hearts.

Once the food was in the bowl, it wasn't long before she had polished off the entire contents, like licking the spoon clean, as well as the floor nearby in case any morsels had inadvertently dropped there.

There was a general consensus that her diet could start again tomorrow.

Also, what a tale we would have to tell our friends in the local coffee shops as well as in the micropub next Thursday, where it could get a bit raucous.

One thought then suddenly occurred to me and judging by the looks of disbelief and shaking of heads, it should have stayed in my head.

Nevertheless, I still chose to voice it.

Now then, where shall we take Peggy for a walk tomorrow?

Our cocker spaniel was in no position to comment, judging from the blissful snores emanating from her favourite spot on the sofa.

Could a duvet day be on the cards?

Later on, we were sitting around the table tucking into one of Rebecca's delicious winter warmers. If my memory serves me right, the winner of series 4 on *'MasterChef'* cooked this on her way to the final.

The dish in question was sausage casserole. With heaps of mustard mash, honey-glazed carrots, and a lovely warming red wine jus.

John Torode would certainly be commenting on how fluffy the buttery mash was.

What a lucky man I am.

It also seems rude not to open a bottle of sparkling fizz with another one on ice.

As a family, we were as content as we ever had been in each other's company counting our blessings after the events of the day, thinking how much worse it could have been.

I know what could top this off.

One more cheeky little snifter of Highland malt.

Peggy

You would not believe the day I've had. It all started pretty well with a dash upstairs to show them my favourite duck toy and grab a few minutes of extra nap on Ernest's bed before he went to work.

Then it was breakfast followed by a few extra treats hidden in a toy that I had to push around with my nose to release the contents. Although that breakfast is a bit boring now, I think I'll take the box for a full English tomorrow.

Anyway, once they'd put my harness on, we'd gone through the 15-minute pantomime of putting on those pesky shoes. I was finally ready for my morning activities.

Note to myself, bury those shoes in the garden next time I get the chance.

Now I can be a bit stubborn at times and personally would have preferred an hour of squirrel chasing in the park. But as it was sunny and Alan was a bit more insistent this time, I thought I'd give this walk a go.

Well, the first part was okay, but my decision to be cooperative was starting to look like a serious error when those loud crashes began, and don't even get me started on the wet stuff coming down. It was just like having a shower at the groomers.

The rest was all a bit of a blur, and I was so chuffed when a nice man in a colourful coat pulled me out of the bushes. I have never been so scared in my life and so desperate for a wee and a poo. So, once I'd completed my ablutions (not a bad word for a cocker spaniel).

I ran up to Alan and covered him in a few smackers, of course, all that left me with a very rumbly tummy and even with the extra treats, in fact, I thought it was just the starter.

All that was left was for me to roll over and let them all give me a thorough belly rub. Then it was time to go to bed and dream of how many squirrels I would chase tomorrow.

"It is great to be back with this lot again."

Dark Clouds

As the evening was drawing in, I was looking out at the clear skies after a warm and sunny afternoon. I had a lovely meal in the resident's dining hall consisting of bangers and mash with a Yorkshire pudding on the side.

After the excitement of the day, I now felt a cosy sense of contentment.

But there was one nagging doubt that suddenly came over me as I spotted a rogue cloud in the distance.

Surely this one and any further showers would have someone else name on it. This particular part of the midlands must have endured enough extreme weather for one day.

I'm sure the lovely weather lady told us that a ridge of high pressure would be setting things down in forth coming days.

But they had also said scattered thundery showers are still possible into the early part of the evening.

With those words still resonating in my subconscious, I was hoping and praying that a certain family were safely behind closed doors. Because from where I'm sitting, I'm sure that rogue black cloud is getting bigger and nearer.